Simon in sum

Gilles Tibo

Tundra Books

My name is Simon and I love summer.

When the sun is warm and the days are long,
I want summer to stay forever.

I go to the pond to look for frogs.

As long as they sing,
Summer will stay.

But when I try to sing with them
They all get scared and jump away.

I walk through lilies to find the Heron,
"How can I make summer last?"

"That's easy, Simon," said the Heron.
"As long as there are flowers there will be butterflies,
As long as there are butterflies,
Summer will last."

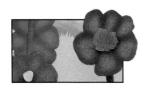

I go to a meadow to look for butterflies.

Marlene brings colored paper and I bring scissors.
We make giant flowers to please the butterflies.

But the butterflies know they are not real flowers.

I go to the pasture to talk to the Cow,
"How can I keep summer from ending?"

"That's easy, Simon," said the Cow.
"As long as the sun is high in the sky,
Summer days will never end."

I go up a hill to get close to the sun.

But the sun moves away and I cannot reach it.

I watch the sun go down
And feel the cool night come.

I cannot keep the frogs singing,
or butterflies on the flowers
or the warm sun high in the sky.

I cannot make summer stay.

But when summer ends all my friends return.

To Vanik

© 1991, Gilles Tibo

Published in Canada by Tundra Books, Montreal, Quebec H3G 1R4
Published in the United States by Tundra Books of Northern New York, Plattsburgh, N.Y. 12901
Distributed in the United Kingdom by Ragged Bears Ltd., Andover, Hampshire SP11 9HX
Distributed in France by Le Colporteur Diffusion, 84100 Orange, France

ISBN 0-88776-261-1 (hardcover) 5 4 3 2 1   Library of Congress Catalog Number: 90-72048

ISBN 0-88776-280-8 (paperback) 5 4 3 2 1

Also available in a French edition, *Simon et le soleil d'été:* ISBN 0-88776-262-X Library of Congress Catalog Number: 90-72049

Canadian Cataloguing in Publication Data
Tibo, Gilles, 1951-
Simon et le soleil d'été.English
        Simon in summer

Issued also in French under title: Simon et le soleil d'été.
ISBN 0-88776-247-6

        I. Title. II. Title: Simon et le soleil d'été. English.

PS8589.I26S53614 1991   jC843'.54   C91-090040-X   PZ7.T42Si 1991

Printed in Hong Kong by South China Printing Co. Ltd.